BEADY BEAR

BY DON FREEMAN

with the Never-Before-Seen Story **Beady's Pillow**

DOVER PUBLICATIONS, INC., MINEOLA, NEW YORK

Don Freeman gave his original draft of *Beady's Pillow* to David's mother, Phyllis Plous. Phyllis handed down this document to us and we have shared it with our children and grandchildren for the past 20 years. We now feel that it is time to share it with all of Don Freeman's readers. We hope that you will cherish the story as much as we have.

Dave and Lisa Plous
2009

Bibliographical Note

Beady Bear: with the Never-Before-Seen Story Beady's Pillow is an unabridged republication of *Beady Bear,* published by The Viking Press in 1954 and reprinted by Penguin Books, New York, in 1981. It includes *Beady's Pillow,* a new work, first published by Dover Publications, Inc., in 2015.

International Standard Book Number
ISBN-13: 978-0-486-79713-7
ISBN-10: 0-486-79713-9

Manufactured in the United States by Courier Corporation
79713901   2015
www.doverpublications.com

BEADY BEAR

Beady was a fuzzy toy bear who belonged to a boy named Thayer.

Hide-and-seek was their favorite fun.

From time to time Beady would suddenly stop and topple over—kerplop! He'd come unwound!

Then Thayer would always go find him and take his key
and gently wind him.

Once Beady was all wound up, he wanted to keep on playing.

And yet when Thayer went to bed Beady knew he ought to, too.

One winter's day Thayer went away. Just when he'd be back
he didn't say.

Being all alone for the first time, Beady amused himself by looking at a book.

"Why hasn't anybody told me this before?" said Beady sadly to himself.

"I wonder if there could be a cave for me away up in those hills?"

Taking a long look through Thayer's shiny telescope he searched
the side of the hill until — he spied

a cave!

So he left a note.

Up the hill he climbed and climbed.

At last!

He could hardly believe his beady eyes — it was just his size!

"A perfect place for a brave bear like me!" sighed Beady.

"And yet it's awfully dark and stilly here inside! And a wee bit chilly, really!"

That night Beady couldn't sleep a wink. "It's because of these sharp stones, I think.

"There's something I need in here to make me truly happy.
I wonder what it could be?"

"Oh, I know!" and up he got and out he trotted down the snowy hillside to his house far below.

And what should he bring back but his very own little pillow!

"This is more like it!" said Beady as he bedded down for the rest of the night.

"But there still seems to be something missing!"

So down the hill he trotted again

and brought back—of all things—a flashlight. But as soon as he settled down he knew

there was something more a bear needed to be truly happy.
"What good is a light without something to read?" said Beady.

The evening papers, indeed!

Now what more could a bear ask for?

Well, after reading all the papers, Beady began to worry and
wonder. "Maybe it's some toys I need..."

At this very moment he heard a loud noise outside.
"It's a bear!" said Beady.

"I must be brave! This is probably his cave!"

The noise grew louder and louder as Beady moved along, ever so slowly and shakily. Suddenly he came to a stop —

and over he toppled — kerplop! "Who's there?" cried Beady,
upside down.

"It's me, Thayer! I'm looking for my bear!"

But from inside the cave now came not a sound — Beady was
much too embarrassed, lying there on the ground!

"Well, hello, Beady boy! I thought I'd find you in this place. That's why I brought along your key, just in case!

"For goodness' sakes, Beady, don't you know you need a key?

"And me?"

"Yes, but if I need you, who do you need?"

"I need Beady!"

So down the hill to home they went, paw in hand and hand in paw,

and when Beady went to bed that night, he was the truly
happiest bear you ever saw.

BEADY'S PILLOW

To the thoughtful little girl
who wondered
if Beady ever found
his Pillow

There once was a boy named Thayer whose best friend was a
fuzzy toy bear.

One day while Thayer was putting on his jacket he said,
"Beady, today I'm going to bring back your pillow.

You left it inside that chilly cave last December, remember?"

"Oh yes," said Beady Bear. "That was the time I climbed up the hill 'cause I wanted to live in a cave same as the other bears."

"But, you came unwound!" said Thayer, "and you toppled over on the ground, and I had to come find you and wind you!"

Beady turned his head. He was still a little embarrassed.

"I won't be gone long," said Thayer kindly. "Here's a new picture puzzle for you to put together while I'm away."

So they nuzzled noses, which is a way some bears have of saying,
"Thank you!"

From the window Beady watched Thayer take his sled and start
trudging up the snow-covered hill.

"I wish I could go along," said Beady sadly. "But my inner spring needs oiling badly."

He took Thayer's shiny telescope in his paws and this is what he saw.

Thayer was just a dot outside the cave.

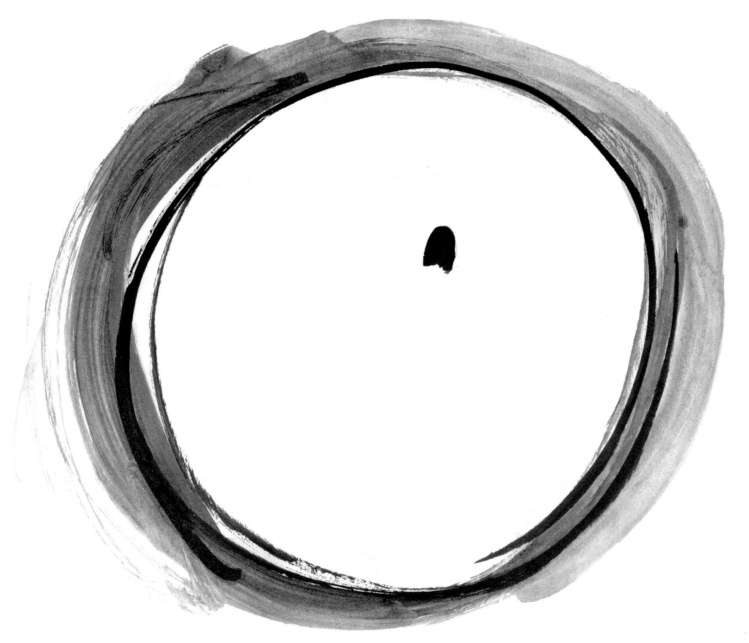

Then he was not.   Anywhere.

"I hope my pillow will still be there!" said Beady as he set aside
the telescope and began putting the pieces of the puzzle together.

When the picture was finished it made him think of Thayer.

He waited and waited. Still his friend didn't appear.
"Oh dear, something must be wrong!"

"I know. He forgot to take along his flashlight!"

Without waiting another minute Beady put on his fluffy wool
muffler and wrote a note to Thayer's mother

and tacked it on the door.

Up the hill he trotted.

But he hadn't gone very far before his inner spring began to squeak.
He was getting mighty weak.

Suddenly he had to stop. No, he didn't topple over Kerplop.
He stood there, not making a move!

Soon he was covered with snow. "I don't want to be a snow bear!"
said Beady. "I want to go find Thayer!"

Just as Beady's nose was about to freeze he felt he had to sneeze!
"Ker — Ker —

—Kerchoo! Oh, s'cuse me!" said Beady politely. The sneeze had done the trick! His inner spring began to click!

And once again he started off to look for his friend.

All this while far inside the cave Thayer was feeling quite lost and foolish. He hadn't yet found Beady's pillow, anywhere!

"It's so dark and truly coolish in here!" he said. "But I won't give up 'till I find what I came for!"

On and on he crawled until finally he thought he saw something slightly white. Was it a rock or a newspaper? Or could it be

Beady's long lost pillow? Yes, indeed it was!

"The stuffings are a bit stiffy," said Thayer as he gave the pillow a tap.
"Still it's soft enough for me to take a nap on. I'm all tuckered out."

But just as he was about to curl up he heard a strange sound!
It came from around the corner.

Thayer tried to hide behind the pillow! "That must be the bear who owns this cave!" he said, his heart beating hard and fast.

All at once a streak of light flashed by! "Who's there?" called
Thayer, very scared.

"It's me, Beady! I'm looking for my friend Thayer who's looking for my pillow!"

"Here I am!" cried Thayer, "and here's your pillow!"

Beady could hardly wait to nuzzle Thayer's nose!

"Don't thank me!" said Thayer. "Thank you, Beady! After all, it was getting awfully dark in here!"

"And you needed your flashlight, didn't you?" asked Beady.

"Indeed I did!" said Thayer as he led the way out of the cave.

Onto the sled they climbed while Beady hugged his pillow tight.

Down the hill to home they glided. Now, did you ever see such a snuggy pair? Anywhere?

That night Thayer decided a certain spring coil deserved a little oiling.

And by the time Beady tumbled into bed his long-gone pillow was
wonderfully warm and soft. Perfect for a brave bear to dream upon.